Flash Harriet
and the Loch Ness Monster

Written by Karen Wallace
Illustrated by Sarah Nayler

◌ Collins

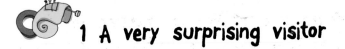

1 A very surprising visitor

Flash Harriet was sitting in her tree house, reading her favourite book. It was called *Daring Detectives* and it was written by her Uncle Proudlock.

Flash Harriet wasn't a piano player like her father, Norman Brilliant, who was famous for his brilliant noise, BOING! BANG! BOING!

She wasn't an acrobat like her mother, Sequin Cynthia, who was famous for taking walks along other people's rooftops.

But Flash Harriet *was* a good detective, just like her Uncle Proudlock, and she was getting better all the time.

The strangest people came to her with the strangest problems and, just like her uncle, she could sort them all out.

Flash Harriet looked across the room to where a large black tarantula was waggling his legs in the air. His name was Gus and he had been Uncle Proudlock's idea. "Best guard dog you can find," Uncle Proudlock had said. He had been right. Gus was always on the case!

Suddenly, a pigeon with a message tied to its leg flew through the tree house window. There was only one person who sent carrier pigeons, and that was Uncle Proudlock! Flash Harriet opened the message on its leg. It said: NEED YOUR HELP. COME AT ONCE. BRING GUS.

Flash Harriet gasped. Uncle Proudlock had never asked for her help before. It must be something very important!

She put Gus into his special travelling box, strapped it to her belt and slid down the firefighter's pole she used for quick exits.

Then she ran across the garden to her house and banged on the window.

"I'm going to Scotland to see Uncle Proudlock!" Flash Harriet shouted over the CRASH! BOOM! of her father's brilliant noises.

Then she waved to her mother, who was standing on her head on top of the chimney.

"Bye-bye, darling!" cried Sequin Cynthia. "Have a lovely time!"

Flash Harriet grinned and waved again.
Nothing her parents did surprised her any more.

Then she jumped onto her motor-powered tricycle and roared off to the station to catch a train.
Uncle Proudlock lived by the side of one of the deepest lakes in Scotland – Loch Ness.

2 A clever plan

"Something odd is happening in Swag Hall," said Uncle Proudlock, as he drove Flash Harriet back to his castle on the edge of Loch Ness. He stopped the car and pointed across the lake to a huge stone house. "When the new people moved in, strange things began to happen."

"What kind of strange things?" asked Flash Harriet. Uncle Proudlock shook his head. "The lights began to go on and off all night and green smoke started to pour out of the chimney."

Uncle Proudlock looked serious. "Then, last week, all the dogs began to bark at the same time. Then all the fish leapt out of the water at the same time. Then all the birds suddenly flew up from the trees."

"At the same time?" Flash Harriet asked, her eyes wide with amazement.

"Yes," replied Uncle Proudlock. "I know it sounds peculiar, but it was as if someone was giving them orders. The dogs and the fish and the birds couldn't stop themselves."

Flash Harriet looked across the lake and saw a huge orange crane fixed to a platform in front of the house. A large hook was hanging over the water. "What's that crane doing there?"

"It arrived last night," said Uncle Proudlock in a serious voice. "That's when I decided I needed your help."

Flash Harriet felt her neck prickle with excitement. "What's the plan?" she asked in her best detective voice.

Uncle Proudlock smiled as he stopped in front of Castle Clue. "How about some early supper, then a trip across the lake in my boat?"

Flash Harriet smiled back. "Sounds good to me."

3 Detectives at work

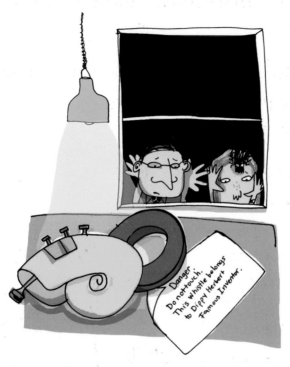

Later that night, Flash Harriet and Uncle Proudlock were peering through the windows of Swag Hall at an empty white room with a table in the middle.

A bright lamp hung from the ceiling and they could see a most odd-looking whistle on the table. There was a card beside it, which said: Danger. Do not touch. This whistle belongs to Dippy Herbert, Famous Inventor.

Flash Harriet shivered. There was something really creepy about the whistle. It looked a bit like a curly seashell, a bit like a trumpet, and a bit like a whistle with an old-fashioned magnet fixed to the end.

Suddenly there was the sound of voices, and Uncle Proudlock and Flash Harriet quickly hid in the bushes.

"So, Mr Claw," said a squeaky voice. "Don't you think I'm clever to invent that whistle?"

In the light of the moon, Flash Harriet
could see a little man with big glasses.
He was standing next to a thin man
who had long straggly hair and a hooked
nose. That must be Mr Claw. Flash Harriet
shivered again, because the thin man had the
nastiest face she had ever seen.

"Oh, shut your mouth, Dippy Herbert, and stop
showing off," snapped a woman in overalls and a
hard hat. "We paid you, didn't we?"

"Shut your mouth yourself, Tight-Fisted Annie," snarled the thin man called Mr Claw. He bent towards her and said in a low voice, "You're here to *steal*, not to think, remember."

"Of course we think you're clever, Dippy," said Mr Claw, smoothly. He turned back to the little inventor. "And by midnight tonight, you will be famous all over the world."

Flash Harriet looked at her watch. Midnight was only an hour away! She looked up at Uncle Proudlock and he nodded as if he was reading her mind. It was time for some fast detective work. The two of them began to creep silently over the grass towards the edge of the lake.

Then suddenly something terrible happened!

Uncle Proudlock tumbled down a deep hole in the ground!

"Uncle Proudlock," whispered Flash Harriet.
She knelt down and peered into the deep hole.
"Are you all right?"

"Don't worry about me!" replied Uncle Proudlock's
voice from the bottom of the hole. "You're a
detective and there's a job to do!"

"But – " cried Flash Harriet.

"No *buts*," ordered Uncle Proudlock. "Find out what that Mr Claw is up to and stop him!"

Flash Harriet knew Uncle Proudlock was right, but she still didn't want to leave him. She took a breath. "I'll come back as fast as I can."

"Good girl," replied Uncle Proudlock's voice. "Now, hurry! There's no time to lose!"

There was a noise of an engine starting up.
Flash Harriet turned. It was coming from some trees behind her. She ran as fast as she could and was just in time to see Tight-Fisted Annie sitting in the driver's seat of a huge truck.

"I'm on my way, Claw!" yelled Tight-Fisted Annie into a walkie-talkie. "I'll hook the monster when it comes up. Just remember! Blow the whistle three times!"

As the huge truck roared down towards the side of the lake, Flash Harriet felt her stomach go cold.

Now she understood what the whistle was for!

Mr Claw and Tight-Fisted Annie were going to kidnap the Loch Ness Monster!

"Hands up, or I'll squirt you with Knock-out Drops," said a squeaky voice.

Flash Harriet spun around. Dippy Herbert was holding a washing-up bottle full of bright pink liquid.

"Mr Claw wants to see you," said Dippy Herbert with a silly smile on his face.

"So I can watch him steal the Loch Ness Monster?" demanded Flash Harriet in a furious voice.

"Don't be stupid," said Dippy Herbert, crossly. "Mr Claw promised me. He just wants to look at the monster."

"With a hook, a crane and a huge truck?" Flash Harriet pulled out her torch. She showed Dippy Herbert a set of deep tyre tracks that could only have been made by a very big truck. "I heard Tight-Fisted Annie talking to Mr Claw," she cried. "They're going to kidnap the monster."

For a moment, Dippy Herbert said nothing. He stared at the tyre tracks. Then he threw down the washing-up bottle and stamped on it. "I've been tricked!" he shouted. "I've been tricked and lied to!"

Dippy Herbert looked up and Flash Harriet could see he was almost in tears. "How can I help you save the monster?" he asked.

"Tell me where Mr Claw is going to blow the whistle from," said Flash Harriet, quickly.

"On the roof at Swag Hall," said Dippy, without hesitation. "Anything else?"

"My Uncle Proudlock is stuck at the bottom of a big hole," said Flash Harriet.

"I know," said Dippy Herbert, sadly. "I dug it."

"Get him out and meet me on the roof as soon as you can!" Harriet shouted. Then she began to run faster than she had ever run in her life.

5 A spider to the rescue

Flash Harriet looked up and saw the outline of Mr Claw in the moonlight. Just as Dippy Herbert had said, he was standing on the flat roof of Swag Hall with the whistle in his hand. She looked down towards the lake. Tight-Fisted Annie was at the controls of the crane, lowering the hook towards the water.

The huge truck was waiting beside the crane with its engine running, ready to go.

Suddenly, the night filled with a weird booming sound. Flash Harriet couldn't believe her ears. Mr Claw was blowing the whistle! A second later, the waters of the lake began to froth and churn, as if something enormous was slowly rising to the surface.

Flash Harriet grabbed the end of the fire escape and began climbing up to the roof as fast as she could.

There was another echoing BOOM, as the whistle blew again.

This time, the waters of the lake began to spin round in a giant whirlpool and the air was filled with leaping fish.

Then Flash Harriet heard her Uncle Proudlock's voice. "Hurry, Flash, hurry! We're coming after you!"

Flash Harriet almost cried out with relief. Uncle Proudlock was free!

But even so, any second now, the evil Mr Claw would blow the whistle for the third time. Only Gus could help her now!

Flash Harriet climbed onto the roof and pulled open the spider's travelling box.

In front of her, Mr Claw was just about to blow the whistle!

"Get him, Gus! Get Claw!" cried Flash Harriet. Then she watched with her heart banging in her chest as Gus leapt through the air and landed on the man's thin, nasty face.

There was a frightened yelp! Then the whistle fell to the ground.

At that moment, Uncle Proudlock and Dippy Herbert jumped onto the roof.

"Quick, Flash!" cried Uncle Proudlock.
"Get the whistle!"

Flash Harriet spun around to see Mr Claw trying to grab the whistle. She bent down, picked it up and threw it into the lake.

The next moment a huge fountain of water rose into the night. The shape of something GIGANTIC glistened in the moonlight.

27

There was an enormous BURP and the SNAP of huge jaws shutting.

Mr Claw gasped and slumped onto the roof.

Nobody else spoke. They couldn't believe what they had seen.

Then Dippy Herbert grabbed Flash Harriet's hand and shook it. Uncle Proudlock patted her shoulder.

"Congratulations, Flash," said Uncle Proudlock, proudly. "You've just saved the Loch Ness Monster!" He grinned. "And thanks to Gus, too!"

Flash Harriet grinned back as Gus landed on her shoulder and tickled her neck with a furry leg. "Good boy," she whispered.

At that moment, a deep, wet gurgle rose from the lake and echoed through the night.

Flash Harriet turned to Uncle Proudlock and gasped.

It sounded just like the monster was laughing underwater!

Gurgle

The clues to the mystery at Swag Hall

1 the lights of Swag Hall going on and off

2 green smoke coming out of the chimney at Swag Hall

3 a group of dogs all barking at once

4 fish leaping out of the lake, as if someone was giving them orders

5 birds flying up from the trees at the same time

6 a huge orange crane fixed to a platform in front of Swag Hall, with the hook hanging over the water of the loch

7 the strange whistle on the table in Swag Hall

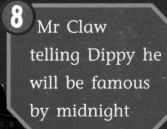

8 Mr Claw telling Dippy he will be famous by midnight

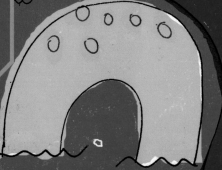

9 Tight-Fisted Annie yelling into a walkie-talkie in the cab of a huge truck

🐾 Ideas for guided reading 🐾

Learning objectives: retell main points of story in sequence; evaluate stories and justify their preferences; refer to significant aspects of the text and know language is used to create these; identify pronouns and understand their functions in sentences; sustain conversation, explaining or giving reasons for their views or choices

Curriculum links: Citizenship: Respect for property; Design and technology: Moving monsters

Interest words: detective, tarantula, loch, motor-powered, peculiar, peering, inventor, magnet, walkie-talkie, kidnap, hesitation, froth, churn, echoing, fountain, glistened, gasped, gurgle

Resources: line graph to plot the story's path

Getting started

This book can be read over two or more guided reading sessions.

- Find out what the children know about the Loch Ness Monster. They could sketch it quickly. Check that they know that *loch* is the Scottish word for *lake*.

- Introduce Flash Harriet by reading the blurb. Ask the group to predict how Harriet's challenge is linked to the Loch Ness Monster.

- Explain that they are going to read chapter 1 first. Ask them to see how many characters are introduced and what they learn about them. Explain how this is the author's way of opening the story.

- Before reading chapter 2 silently, ask the group to predict why it is called 'A clever plan'. Start to plot the events in the story on a line graph, showing how tension is building.

Reading and responding

- As they read the rest of the story, ask them what they notice about the tension in the story? What events and vocabulary have contributed to the spooky atmosphere?